Beauty and the Beast

Bath New York Singapore Hong Kong Cologne Delhi Melbourne

nce upon a time, a selfish young prince refused to give an old beggar-woman shelter in his castle. But the old woman was really an enchantress in disguise. She turned the prince into a terrifying Beast and cast a spell on everyone else in the castle.

Then, giving the Beast a magic rose, she said, "This will bloom until your twenty-first year. If you learn to love another and earn that person's love in return before the last petal falls, the spell will be broken. If not, you will **remain a Beast for ever.**

In a village near the castle, an eccentric inventor named Maurice lived with his beautiful daughter Belle.

One of the young men in the village, Gaston, had decided that he would marry Belle. "After all," he told his friend Lefou, "she's the best-looking girl in town. And I deserve the best!" But Belle refused him. She could never marry someone as arrogant and conceited as Gaston!

One day Maurice set off for a fair with his latest invention. As night fell he lost his way and had to seek refuge in the Beast's castle.

Maurice was welcomed by some friendly enchanted objects, including Lumiere, an elegant candelabra, Cogsworth, a pompous clock, Mrs Potts, a cheery teapot, and her son, Chip, a teacup.

But the Beast was furious when he discovered a stranger in his home, and he threw Maurice in the dungeon.

When Maurice's horse returned home alone, Belle set off at once to search for her father.

"Oh, Papa," Belle cried when she found Maurice in the freezing dungeon, "we must get you out of here!"

Sensing danger, Belle turned round. There was the Beast, towering over her.

"Let my father go," Belle pleaded. "I'll take his place."

The Beast agreed at once. He dragged Maurice out of the cell and sent him back to the village.

The Beast showed Belle to her room. "You can go anywhere in the castle," he told her, "except the West Wing. That is forbidden!"

Poor Belle was so miserable! The enchanted objects tried to cheer her up with their singing and dancing. Even Cogsworth joined in.

But Belle was still lonely and later that night she wandered through the castle. Soon she was in the West Wing. There, among broken furniture, ripped clothes and cracked mirrors, she found the magic rose, its petals drooping sadly.

Just as Belle reached out to touch the rose, the Beast burst in, howling with rage. Terrified, Belle ran out into the snowy night.

Belle leapt onto her father's horse and set off into the forest. Suddenly, she was surrounded by a pack of vicious, hungry wolves.

Just as the wolves closed in for the kill, the Beast appeared. Fighting bravely, he drove the wolves away, but then he sank to the ground in pain.

Back at the castle, Belle tended the Beast's wounds. He seemed different now, and she was no longer frightened of him.

Meanwhile, at the village tavern, Gaston was still brooding over Belle.

Suddenly, the door burst open and Maurice raced in.

"Help!" he cried. "Belle's being held prisoner by a monstrous **Beast!**"

The men in the tavern burst out laughing. They thought Maurice was mad! But Gaston smiled to himself. He had thought of a way to make Belle marry him!

As the days passed, Belle and the Beast spent more and more time together. The enchanted objects were delighted. They were certain that Belle would fall in love with their master and break the spell.

But time was running out. Each day a few more petals fell from the magic rose.

One evening the Beast and Belle sat together on the terrace.

"Are you happy here, Belle?" asked the Beast.

"Yes," replied Belle. "I just wish I could see my father again."

"You can," said the Beast, giving Belle a magic mirror. "This will show you whatever you wish."

In it, Belle saw her father lost in the forest, trembling with cold as he searched for Belle!

"I must help him!" cried Belle.

Although the Beast loved Belle, he knew he had to let her go to her father. "Take the mirror with you," he said, "so you can remember me."

With the mirror's help, Belle soon found Maurice. She brought him safely home and nursed him back to health.

The next day Gaston arrived at Belle's house with a crowd of villagers. He said Maurice would be taken to an asylum unless Belle agreed to marry him.

"My father's not mad!" cried Belle.

"He must be," said Lefou. "He was raving about a huge beast!"

"The Beast is real!" cried Belle. "Look!" She held up the magic mirror, and the crowd saw the Beast for themselves.

Furious that his plan had failed, Gaston gathered a mob to attack the Beast's castle.

Cogsworth led the enchanted objects in a spirited defence of the castle. But the Beast missed Belle and was too heartbroken to fight, even when Gaston beat him with a club and drove him onto the roof. Only when he heard Belle's voice did the Beast look up.

"You came back!" he cried, rushing to embrace Belle.

This was the chance Gaston had been waiting for. Drawing his dagger, he stabbed the beast in the back. But as the Beast collapsed, Gaston tripped and fell, tumbling from the roof.

Belle ran to the Beast and bent to kiss him. The last rose petal was about to fall.

"You can't die," sobbed Belle. "I love you!"

Suddenly, a magic mist surrounded the Beast, and before Belle's astonished eyes he changed into the handsome young prince he once had been.

One by one, the enchanted objects became human again. Weeping with joy, they hugged each other as the Prince swept Belle into his arms.

The Prince had found his true love at last, and the enchantress's spell was broken. As the sun burst through the clouds, they knew they would all live in happiness for ever after.